Much Ado About Nothing

Sweet Cherry
Publishing

Published by Sweet Cherry Publishing Limited
Unit E, Vulcan Business Complex,
Vulcan Road,
Leicester, LE5 3EB,
United Kingdom

First published in the USA in 2013
ISBN: 978-1-78226-074-5

©Macaw Books

Title: Much Ado About Nothing
North American Edition

Text & Illustration by Macaw Books 2013

www.sweetcherrypublishing.com

Printed and bound by Wai Man Book Binding (China) Ltd. Kowloon, H.K.

About Shakespeare

William Shakespeare, regarded as the greatest writer in the English language, was born in Stratford-upon-Avon in Warwickshire, England (around April 23, 1564). He was the third of eight children born to John and Mary Shakespeare.

Shakespeare was a poet, playwright, and dramatist. He is often known as England's national poet and the "Bard of Avon." Thirty-eight plays, 154 sonnets, two long narrative poems, and several other poems are attributed to him. Shakespeare's plays have been translated into every major existent language and are performed more often than those of any other playwright.

Beatrice: She is Hero's cousin and Leonato's niece. She is witty, generous, rebellious, and good-hearted. She often uses her wit to mock people. Even though she appears tough, she is quite vulnerable.

Benedick: He is a lord and soldier from Padua. He has just returned from war. He is witty and, just like Beatrice, likes mocking people. He is willing to help others and speaks openly about injustice done to anyone.

Claudio: He is a young gentleman who has also returned from war. He falls in love with Hero, daughter of Leonato. However, in the play, he is easily fooled regarding Hero's disloyalty and is hasty in punishing her.

Don John: He is the brother of Claudio and the villain of the play. He plots a dark scheme to ruin the happiness of Hero and Claudio.

Much Ado About Nothing

Leonato was the governor at the palace in the city of Messina. He had a daughter by the name of Hero, who lived with him, and also a niece called Beatrice. Of the two cousins,

Beatrice was the one with a lively temper, and she was always playing pranks on the more sober Hero.

One day, some old friends of Leonato were passing through the city, and they decided to pay him a visit. These men were returning to their own lands, having fought a gruesome war a short distance from Messina. The first man was Don Pedro, the Prince of Arragon; the second was Claudio, the Lord of Florence; and the third was Benedick, the Lord of Padua.

9

Leonato warmly welcomed
them and introduced them to
his now grown-up daughter
and niece. Benedick, the Lord
of Padua, was a lively man and
was soon engaged in a discussion
with his host about the just
concluded war. Meanwhile,

Beatrice was getting bored sitting out of the conversation and was trying her best to participate. After some time, she could not resist saying, "You do talk a lot... Do you think

people are even listening to you?"

Benedick was very similar in character to Beatrice, but he did not think that this interruption in his conversation with Leonato was very ladylike. In the past, he and Beatrice had played pranks on each other, and every time, Benedick had left with a quiet murmur of displeasure. This time he was not amused by Beatrice's

rude remark, and unable
to hold back, he exclaimed,
"Oh, are you still here?"

Needless to say, this brought
about a huge war of words
between them. The fight took
different turns until Beatrice
told Benedick that she would

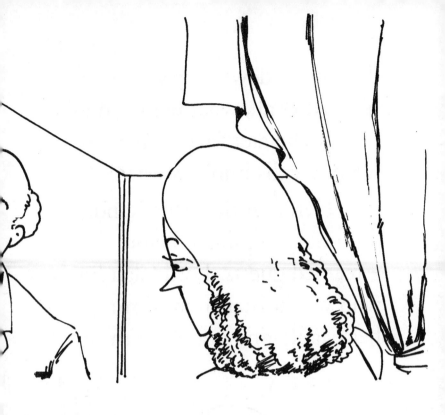

eat all that he had killed in the
war. She went on to call him the
prince's jester. It was well known
to all present that Benedick had
shown his valor in
the just concluded
war, and therefore,
Beatrice's accusation

did not go down very well with him. After all, what man can take calmly the fact that a frivolous woman calls him a coward?

Hero, on the other hand, did not speak much before the esteemed guests. Lord Claudio, who was at that time admiring her beauty and grace, overheard

the fight between Benedick and Beatrice. He could not help breaking into a smile and told Leonato how Beatrice and Benedick would make a perfect match. To this, Leonato remarked that

in the event they were married, they would drive each other mad in a week just by talking to each other. Claudio, however, did not dismiss the idea altogether.

As Benedick and Claudio returned from the palace, Claudio could not stop talking about Hero's charm and elegance, and how she had captivated him completely. This got Benedick thinking that perhaps there could be a matrimonial alliance between his friend Claudio and the noble Hero. Upon asking

whether he was in love with Hero, Claudio only replied that before he had looked upon her merely as a soldier, with no leisure for loving.

But now that they were in times of peace, he had softer thoughts about her.

Benedick immediately realized
that Claudio was in love with
Hero, and immediately went to
Leonato and proposed the issue
of Claudio's marriage to her.
Leonato did not seem opposed
to the idea. Hero's consent was
easily obtained, for Claudio
was truly one of the most
accomplished men the world had

ever seen. Benedick then fixed
an early date for the marriage.

Soon, it was time for the
wedding. Though there were
only a few days left, Claudio felt
that time stood still. Don Pedro,
sensing his friend's anxious
state of mind, decided to create

a pastime to take his mind off
his despair. He suggested that
in those few days they should
do something that would help

Benedick and Beatrice grow
closer and fall in love. Claudio,
who had already thought of the
matter earlier, decided to join
the prince in his scheme. When
Leonato was informed, he too
assured them of his cooperation,
and Hero also agreed, willing
to do anything for her cousin.

Finally, they drew up a plan between themselves—the men were to make Benedick believe that Beatrice was in love with him, while it was Hero's task to make sure Beatrice believed Benedick was in love with her.

They decided to put the plan into

action at once. The men said
that they would make the first
move and went out in search
of Benedick. They found him
sitting all by himself, reading
in a quiet little place away from
the palace. They took up their
positions behind some trees near
the unsuspecting Benedick. After

some casual conversation, Don
Pedro started by asking Leonato,
"Now what were you telling
me—that Beatrice is actually

in love with Benedick?" Leonato continued with the game and explained how he had found out about her love for the Lord of Padua. Claudio also played his part by confirming the news. "Yes, Hero told me about it, too. She said that if Benedick were to go away, she would surely die of grief."

Making sure that Benedick could hear them, Don Pedro

continued and told his friends
how Benedick should be informed.

But Claudio cut
in and said that
there was no point
in telling him
anything because he
would merely use
it to taunt Beatrice
further. To this, Don
Pedro retorted, "If
he were to play with
her heart he should
be hanged, because
she is truly a noble
and gentle lady."

When they
finished their
conversation,

Don Pedro motioned his
friends to move away and
leave Benedick to think
about what they had said.

Their words had not fallen on
deaf ears, and Benedick wondered
if it could indeed be true.
He reasoned with himself that
Beatrice was truly a gentle soul,

and since Claudio had heard it from Hero, it had to be true.

While Benedick was pondering the matter, Beatrice arrived and said, "Much against my own will, I have been sent here to ask you to come in for dinner." Previously, her rude statements might have offended

Benedick, but this time he calmly
replied, "My dear Beatrice, thank
you for taking the trouble." She
tried to speak to him rudely
again, but Benedick was sure
there were traces of love
veiled within her speech.
    Now that the men
had done their part,
it was time for Hero

to convince Beatrice
that Benedick was
in love with her.
She immediately
requested the help of
her two friends, Ursula and
Margaret. To Margaret, she said,
"Go in and find Beatrice. Tell
her that Ursula and I are talking

about her in the orchard." Once Margaret left, Hero turned to Ursula and told her about the plan. She said, "Whenever I mention Benedick, you should praise him to the skies. We will have to convince her that Benedick is in love with her. Here she comes…Let's begin!"

They followed the same process as the men. Hero kept telling Ursula that it would be better if Beatrice never got to know about Benedick's feelings, as she would just make fun of him. And Ursula kept talking about Benedick's merits, saying that he was the finest

man in the whole of Italy. Their conversation had the desired effect on Beatrice, who listened with bated breath. Finally, she told herself, "If he loves me so, then I too will love him."

Soon, the bitter enemies were turned into sweet lovers. But alas, good times do not

last long. The next day was
Hero's marriage to Claudio,
and it turned out to be one of
the darkest days in her life.

Don John, Don Pedro's brother, came to Messina that day. He was a rogue and different from his brother in every way. He hated Claudio because he was Don Pedro's close friend. He wanted to have the wedding stopped by any means necessary,

and so sent his man Borachio to court Margaret and have her do his bidding.
That night, under Borachio's instructions, Margaret dressed herself in Hero's clothes and 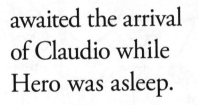 awaited the arrival of Claudio while Hero was asleep.

Don John then went to Claudio and told him how he had seen Hero talking to another man under the cover of darkness. This came as a shock to Claudio, and he took an oath

that if this were truly the case, he would insult Hero the next day at their wedding. Don Pedro also decided to join Claudio if Don John was speaking the truth.

So, when Don John brought the angry lords to Hero's chambers, they saw "her" speaking to Borachio. Claudio's love was now immediately

converted to hatred for the
innocent Hero, and he and
Don Pedro decided to go
ahead and disgrace her in
the church the next day.

Finally, the day of the
grand wedding arrived, and
Hero and Claudio, with their

friends, assembled at the
church before the Holy Friar.
But before proceedings could
begin, Claudio rebuked Hero
in the vilest way
possible. Hero and
Leonato could
not believe what

they were hearing, and Hero could only ask meekly, "Are you feeling all right, my lord, that you speak to me so?"

Claudio told the people gathered there about what he had seen the previous night. Benedick could not believe it. He knew Hero to be good and was certain

that Claudio must
be mistaken. But
Hero could not
bear the attack on
her character, and

she fell to the floor unconscious.
So crestfallen was she that the
color drained from her face, as if
she were dead. But Claudio and

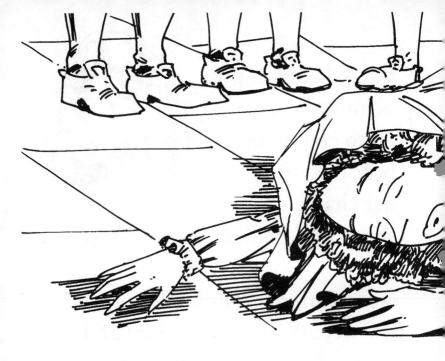

Don Pedro simply walked off, while Benedick stood beside poor Hero and her distraught father.

Now the friar who was conducting the wedding knew from the look on Hero's face that she had indeed been speaking the truth. So he thought of a plan. As Hero regained

consciousness, he told Leonato
that he should spread the news
that Hero had died. He even
asked him to
organize a burial
for her, as then
the truth about
Claudio's feelings
would surely
come out.

Beatrice loved her cousin Hero, and knew that all that had been said about her that night was false. She therefore urged her lover, Benedick, to challenge Claudio to a duel for having insulted her cousin. Benedick obviously did not want to draw swords against his good friend, but he could not stand to see Beatrice in such a terrible state. After much consideration, he decided to fight Claudio.

But before the two friends could actually draw their swords, some good news arrived, which solved everyone's problem for the time being. The local magistrate had heard Borachio bragging about how he had succeeded in fooling Claudio.

From him they learned the
whole story about Don John's
plans and how it had been not
Hero but her friend Margaret
at the window that night.

Claudio was very ashamed of
himself. He rushed to the palace
to ask for Hero's forgiveness, when

Leonato informed him that Hero
had died. This broke Claudio's
heart, as he blamed himself
for her death. Leonato
decided to continue
with the plan, and said,
"Well, if you repent
of your actions, I
will ask you to

marry one of Hero's cousins. Are you willing, Claudio?"

Claudio obviously had no other option but to agree to the proposal. So it was decided that Claudio and Hero's cousin would get married the next day.

When Claudio arrived at the church, he was married to a

woman whose face was
hidden by a veil. As
the marriage ceremony
was concluded,
Claudio turned to her
and said, "Madam, to you
I will be your husband for this
whole life of mine." The lady
removed her veil and asked,

58

"As you have been my husband in my earlier life?"

Claudio could not believe his eyes. His beloved Hero was standing there in front of him. It was then that Benedick told him of the plan they had made after Claudio and Don Pedro left the church in a huff.

Don John, who had run away from Messina after Borachio was

caught by the magistrate, was later apprehended and brought back to the city. He was given a rigorous punishment on account of what he had done.

Soon, Benedick and Beatrice were also married. Only then did their friends tell them about

the plan they had devised to get them to fall in love. But it did not matter any more, for Beatrice and Benedick were very much in love and could not live without each other.

While the happy people were left alone, Benedick turned to the crowd and said, "Well, finally everything has worked out for the best." And Claudio added, "Yes, we all played tricks

on each other and yet here we are all together now. That is all that matters."

Leonato, upon seeing his daughter and niece

happily married to two noble young men, could not help but declare at the very end of it all, "Yes, there was much ado about nothing. I'm glad it is all in the past now."